HELLO KITTY®

and

♥•ME•♥

Trick or Treat

Published by Sourcebooks Jabberwocky, an imprint of Sourcebooks, Inc.
P.O. Box 4410, Naperville, Illinois 60567-4410
(630) 961-3900
Fax: (630) 961-2168
www.jabberwockykids.com

Library of Congress Cataloging-in-Publication data is on file with the publisher.

Source of Production: Worzalla, Stevens Point WI, USA
Date of Production: May 2014
Run Number: 5001675

Printed and bound in the United States of America.
WOZ 10 9 8 7 6 5 4 3 2 1

It's Halloween! Hello Kitty and her twin sister, Mimmy, are so excited. They just picked out their pumpkins.

Hello Kitty and Mimmy are having a costume party for their friends. Fifi is dressed up like a pirate. *Ahoy!*

Dear Daniel is going as a monster. *Spooky!*

Thomas, Jodie, and Tippy are all dressed up like vampires.

But Hello Kitty and Mimmy can't decide what to be. What do you like to be on Halloween?

Hello Kitty and Mimmy help
Mama make cookies for the
Halloween party.

Papa is in charge of decorations. What do you think Papa is making?

Hello Kitty and Mimmy still
don't know what they will be.
It's so hard to choose!

Suddenly, Hello Kitty and Mimmy have the same idea! What do you think they will be?

Mama is working on the costumes. Papa is making a surprise. No peeking, Hello Kitty and Mimmy!

Now the costumes are all finished. Don't they look cute?

Everyone is here. Hooray!

First, they all go trick-or-treating.
They fill up their bags with candy.

Then it's time for the party.
Papa shows off his surprise:
Halloween cupcakes!

Hello Kitty and Mimmy think two witches are twice as nice as one. Come join the Halloween party!

Happy Halloween!

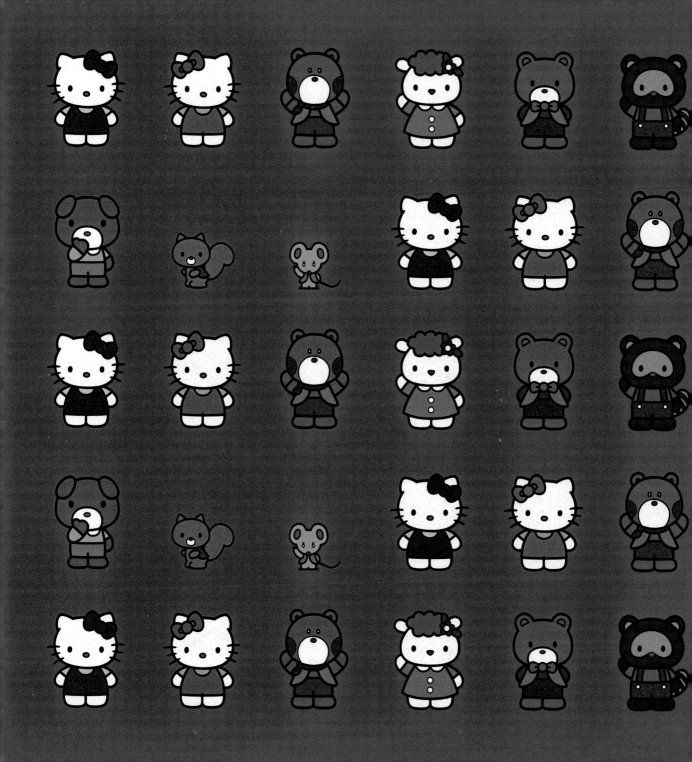